W9-BYH-673

For Federica, who received such love from her own mother that she became a wonderful and tender mom herself.

Library of Congress Cataloging-in-Publication Data available.

ISBN 978-1-4521-7190-6

Manufactured in China.

Design by Maggie Edelman.
Typeset in Archer.

10 9 8 7 6 5 4 3 2 1

Chronicle Books LLC
680 Second Street
San Francisco, California 94107

Chronicle Books—we see things differently.
Become part of our community at www.chroniclekids.com.

MOM and Me, Me and MOM

Miguel Tanco

chronicle books · san francisco

I help you wake up . . .

and I change your mood.

POST

I test your flexibility . . .

and your reflexes.

VOGU

I show you how to look neat . . .

and how to be messy.

I help you see nature . . .

and hear it.

I show you how to see
things differently . . .

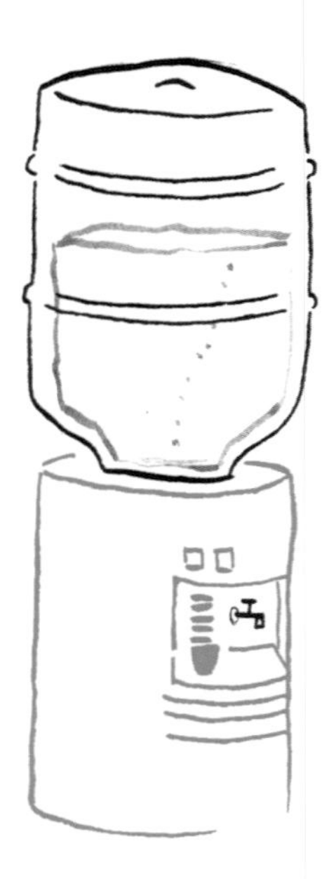

and I introduce you to new friends.

I follow your lead . . .

and keep your secrets safe.

I help you take giant leaps . . .

and even though I am small,
I show you how to look further.